P9-DNO-017

WITHDRAWN
LVC BISHOP LIBRARY

The Secret Shofar of Barcelona

Jacqueline Dembar Greene

Illustrated by Doug Chayka

KAR-BEN
PUBLISHING

To my Sephardic grandparents,
who kept the faith—and the foods!   J.D.G.

With thanks to the Levine family   D.C.

Text copyright © 2009 by Jacqueline Dembar Greene
Illustrations copyright © by Lerner Publishing Group

All rights reserved. International copyright secured. No part of this book may
be reproduced, stored in a retrieval system, or transmitted in any form or by any
means—electronic, mechanical, photocopying, recording, or otherwise—without prior
written permission of Lerner Publishing Group, Inc., except for the inclusion of brief
quotations in an acknowledged review.

KAR-BEN PUBLISHING
A division of Lerner Publishing Group, Inc.
241 First Avenue North
Minneapolis, MN 55401 U.S.A.
1-800-4KARBEN

Website address: www.karben.com

Library of Congress Cataloging-in-Publication Data

Greene, Jacqueline Dembar.

  The secret shofar of Barcelona / by Jacqueline Dembar Greene ; illustrated by Doug
Chayka.

    p. cm.

  Summary: In the late 1500s, while Don Fernando, conductor of the Royal Orchestra
of Barcelona, prepares for a concert to celebrate Spain's colonies in the New World,
his son Rafael secretly practices playing the shofar for the Jews, who must hide their
faith from the Inquisition, to celebrate Rosh Hashanah, the Jewish New Year. Includes
historical facts and glossary.

  ISBN 978-0-8225-9915-9 (lib. bdg. : alk. paper) 1. Marranos--Spain--Fiction. 2. Jews-
-Spain--History--16th century--Juvenile fiction. [1. Marranos--Fiction. 2. Jews--Spain--
Fiction. 3. Concerts--Fiction. 4. Shofar--Fiction. 5. Rosh ha-Shanah--Fiction. 6. Spain--
History--Philip II, 1556-1598--Fiction.] I. Chayka, Doug, ill. II. Title.

  PZ7.G834Sec 2009

  [Fic]--dc22   2008031197

Manufactured in the United States of America
1 2 3 4 5 6 – DP – 09 10 11 12 13 14

In 1492, Queen Isabella and King Ferdinand decreed that everyone in Spain must be Catholic. Those of other faiths were forced to leave the country or to convert. Most Jews sailed for other lands. Some remained and pretended to follow Catholic ways. For many generations, these "conversos" hid their religion from the Inquisition, a board of judges set up to find anyone who did not follow the Church's teachings. Spies were everywhere, and the secret Jews lived in fear of being discovered.

Rafael stepped silently into the music room. The notes of the harpsichord plinked under his father's fingertips. When the final chord faded away, Rafael clapped. "Bravo, Papa! Did you write a new piece?" he asked.

Don Fernando smiled. "After I convinced the Duke to hold a concert celebrating Spain's colonies in the New World, I had to compose something never heard before."

He led Rafael to a cluttered table. "These instruments were made by the natives, and I have written a part for each one."

Rafael jiggled a string of clattering black triangles. "Those are deer toes," Don Fernando explained. Rafael shook gourd rattles, beat on small drums, and tipped a hollow log that made the silvery sound of rainfall.

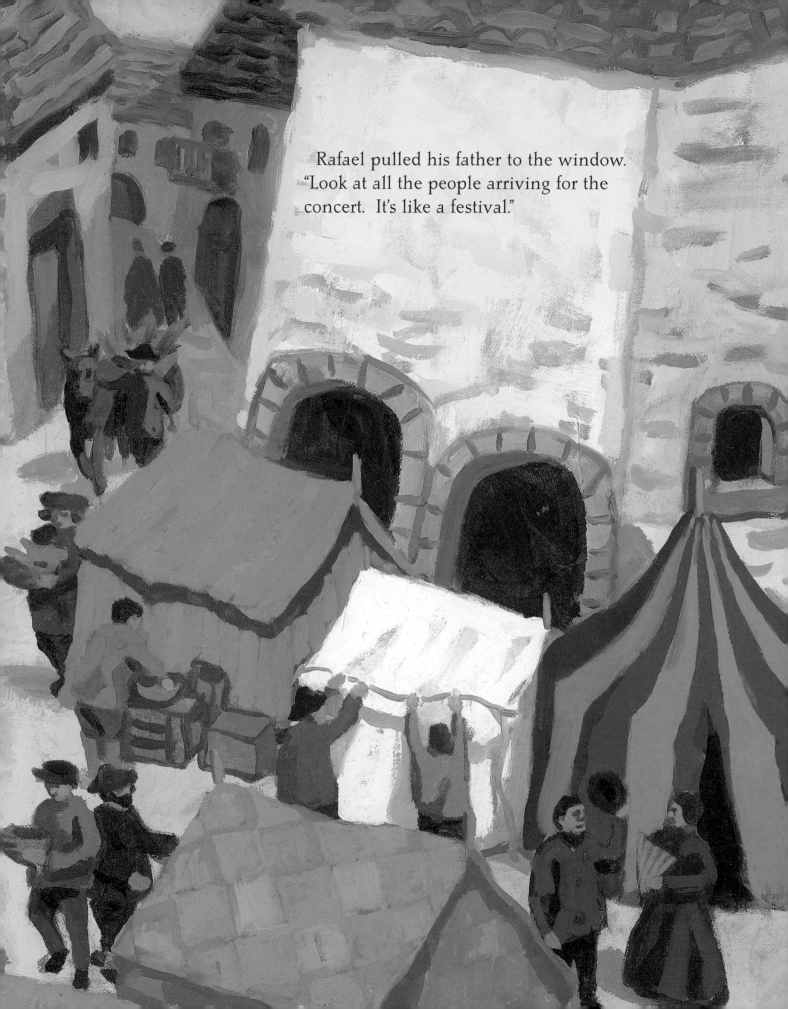

Rafael pulled his father to the window. "Look at all the people arriving for the concert. It's like a festival."

A housemaid walked past the door and Don Fernando lowered his voice. "The concert marks another celebration, but that one is a secret."

"Tell me, Papa," Rafael whispered. He had been trusted with many secrets. Most important was hiding his family's Jewish faith.

Don Fernando played the harpsichord louder to muffle his words. "The performance will be on the first night of Rosh Hashanah, the Jewish New Year. When we and our Jewish friends gather for a festive meal, it will appear we are only celebrating the concert."

Rafael knew the plan was dangerous. Don Fernando was the respected conductor of the Royal Orchestra of Barcelona, but nothing would protect him if the Inquisition discovered his trick.

Rafael had an idea. "Since it is Rosh Hashanah, you could add the call of the shofar to the native instruments."

Don Fernando's shoulders slumped. "So many of Barcelona's Jews have longed to hear it. But who would take such a risk?"

"I will," Rafael said. "If you are brave enough to conduct a Rosh Hashanah concert in front of the Duke and the Inquisition, then I will play the shofar." He gave his father a sly smile. "Maybe it's safest to hide the shofar in plain sight."

"Perhaps you are right," Don Fernando said thoughtfully.
He unlocked a cabinet and slid out a wooden box. Beneath
a velvet cover was a curved ram's horn.

"Listen carefully," Don Fernando said.
He softly sang a pattern of four notes.
Rafael hummed them back until they
were safely locked in his memory.

The next morning, Rafael slipped the shofar under his shirt. He made sure no one followed him as he walked to the olive groves. Only the grazing sheep could hear him practice. At first, his breath was short, but soon the sounds grew stronger.

The notes his father had revealed seemed to speak to Rafael. *Teki'ah*, was a long, whole note. Would the secret Jews of Barcelona feel whole again if they heard it?

The three broken notes of *shevarim* reminded him that the tradition of sounding the shofar had been broken. Perhaps this year it would be restored.

Rafael felt a sense of alarm each time he played the blaring *teru'ah*. The nine rapid notes seemed to be a warning call.

The last, great blast -- called the *teki'ah gedolah,* the great *teki'ah* -- echoed in his heart.

While Rafael practiced, he worried. What if the Duke or the Inquisition recognized the ancient ram's horn? Rafael and his father would be thrown into prison—or worse.

At sundown the day of the concert, trusted friends
gathered in Don Fernando's library to welcome the
New Year. Some prayed quietly, while others talked
loudly to cover the sound of prayers.

Rafael's mother lit candles in the dining room, secretly reciting a blessing. So many traditions were hidden in plain sight.

They feasted on chicken simmered with olives and tomatoes, rice with bits of dates and apricots, and round loaves of bread laced with raisins. But Rafael was too nervous to eat.

Later they walked the winding narrow streets to the palace courtyard alongside a crowd of elegantly dressed men and women. Men placed their hats over their hearts to show their respect for Don Fernando.

Lanterns flickered at the edge of the stage as the musicians took their places. Rafael felt a shiver of fear. He climbed onto the platform clutching the shofar. His throat went dry. What if the plan failed?

Don Fernando stepped onto the
stage. At his signal, the music
began. After several familiar
pieces, the orchestra began the
new composition. It opened with
a gentle rhythm, and grew louder
and faster. Gourds rattled, clay
flutes piped, and deer toes clacked.
With a flourish, Don Fernando
pointed. Rafael put the shofar to his
lips and blew.

*Tek'iah! Shevarim! Teru'ah! Tek'iah
Gedolah!* Rafael blew the last note
until he thought his chest would
burst. He wanted the sound to
reach every secret Jew in Barcelona.

"Bravo!" The people jumped to their feet. The musicians bowed as fireworks exploded against the night sky.

"Tonight, you have made many hearts sing," Don Fernando whispered to his son. "Especially mine."

Suddenly, a messenger appeared. "The Duke wishes to see you—and the young horn player," he told Don Fernando. Rafael gripped his father's hand as they followed the messenger to the royal box.

They bowed before the Duke and the judges of the Inquisition. Rafael's heart seemed to stop.

"That is a strange horn the boy played," the Duke said. "Let me see it."

Trembling, Rafael offered the shofar. The Duke raised it to his lips and blew. *"Blattt!"* He frowned at the sour note. "I am afraid I shall never be a musician."

The Duchess chuckled. "That is why we have our famous Don Fernando and his orchestra."

The Duke's expression softened. "The concert was an inspiring tribute to our valiant *conquistadors,*" he said. "You must perform this music again. And you shall blow this horn."

He returned the shofar to Rafael.

"Next year, at the very same time," Rafael agreed. "Right before your eyes."

Author's Note

Barcelona in the late 1500s was a city of merchants, farmers, and shopkeepers. Many were *conversos*, Jews who pretended to be Catholics, but secretly practiced their faith.

So it happened that a story grew about a courageous *converso* named Don Fernando Aguilar. It is said that he was either a famous composer, or the conductor of the Royal Orchestra of Barcelona. While such a man may have lived, there is no mention of him in history books. Nor is there record of a Royal Orchestra. But music was an important part of Spanish life. Almost everyone learned to play guitar. People sang, and loved hearing ballads and poems set to music. Wealthy families kept musicians in their palaces for entertainment. Often, noblemen would declare a festival and present a concert. Travelers came from long distances to camp in the fields and celebrate.

On the night of the concert, the wealthy sat in chairs, while the common people stood at the back. When the music ended, a display of fireworks dazzled the crowd.

According to legend, Don Fernando decided to secretly honor the Jewish New Year by presenting a concert that included the blowing of the shofar. How did his trick escape detection? Perhaps, as my version of this tale recounts, it was because he and his son hid the shofar in plain sight.